Lion Manes

Tracy Kompelien

Illustrated by Anne Haberstroh

Consulting Editor, Diane Craig, M.A./Reading Specialist

ABDO
Publishing Company

Published by ABDO Publishing Company, 4940 Viking Drive, Edina, Minnesota 55435.

Printed in the United States.

Credits
Edited by: Pam Price
Curriculum Coordinator: Nancy Tuminelly
Cover and Interior Design and Production: Mighty Media
Photo Credits: Brand X Pictures, Digital Vision, ShutterStock

Library of Congress Cataloging-in-Publication Data

Kompelien, Tracy, 1975-
    Lion manes / Tracy Kompelien ; illustrated by Anne Haberstroh.
        p. cm. -- (Fact & fiction. Animal tales)
    Includes index.
    Summary: Laura Lion envies the handsome new mane her best friend Leo grows over the summer, but when she tries to match his achievement, disaster strikes. Contains facts about lions.
    ISBN 1-59679-949-8 (hardcover)
    ISBN 1-59679-950-1 (paperback)
    [1. Friendship--Fiction. 2. Lions--Fiction.] I. Haberstroh, Anne, ill. II. Title. III. Series.

PZ7.K83497Li 2006
[E]--dc22
                                                                            2005024447

SandCastle Level: Fluent

SandCastle™ books are created by a professional team of educators, reading specialists, and content developers around five essential components—phonemic awareness, phonics, vocabulary, text comprehension, and fluency—to assist young readers as they develop reading skills and strategies and increase their general knowledge. All books are written, reviewed, and levels for guided reading, early reading intervention, and Accelerated Reader® programs for use in shared, guided, and independent reading and writing activities to support a balanced approach to literacy instruction. The SandCastle™ series has four levels that correspond to early literacy development. The levels help teachers and parents select appropriate books for young readers.

Emerging Readers	**Beginning Readers**	**Transitional Readers**	**Fluent Readers**
(no flags)	(1 flag)	(2 flags)	(3 flags)

These levels are meant only as a guide. All levels are subject to change.

FACT & FICTION

This series provides early fluent readers the opportunity to develop reading comprehension strategies and increase fluency. These books are appropriate for guided, shared, and independent reading.

FACT The left-hand pages incorporate realistic photographs to enhance readers' understanding of informational text.

FICTION The right-hand pages engage readers with an entertaining, narrative story that is supported by whimsical illustrations.

The Fact and Fiction pages can be read separately to improve comprehension through questioning, predicting, making inferences, and summarizing. They can also be read side-by-side, in spreads, which encourages students to explore and examine different writing styles.

FACT OR FICTION? This fun quiz helps reinforce students' understanding of what is real and not real.

SPEED READ The text-only version of each section includes word-count rulers for fluency practice and assessment.

GLOSSARY Higher-level vocabulary and concepts are defined in the glossary.

SandCastle™ would like to hear from you.

Tell us your stories about reading this book. What was your favorite page? Was there something hard that you needed help with? Share the ups and downs of learning to read. To get posted on the ABDO Publishing Company Web site, send us an e-mail at:

sandcastle@abdopublishing.com

Young lion cubs spend a lot of their time playing. Their playing helps them develop survival skills such as stalking and fighting.

Laura and Leo have been best friends since they were young cubs. They learned to pounce, growl, and hunt together. They were very much alike.

Lions' long tails help them balance. The lion is the only kind of cat with a tassel at the tip of its tail.

Laura hasn't seen Leo all summer, so she can't wait to see him today.

Ring! The doorbell chimes, and Laura leaps to the door. "Hi, Laura!" Leo roars happily.

Laura stares. Leo has a beautiful, new mane! They are not alike anymore.

7

Most cats eat standing up, but lions eat crouching or lying down. Lions are carnivores.

Laura loves Leo's new look. She decides that
if she eats a lot of vegetables, she can grow
a mane like Leo's. Laura eats and eats, but she
does not grow a mane.

A lion's roar can be heard up to five miles away. Lions roar to let the other lions in the pride know where they are or to scare off lions that don't belong.

Laura rides her scooter over to Manes on Main, where Harry the hair guru works. "Harry," she cries, "can you help me grow a mane?"

Harry roars with laughter, "Oh Laura, you'll never grow a mane. But you can buy one. Take a look over there."

11

Lions' eyes are very large and yellow. They have a special coating that helps lions to see well even when there is little light.

Inside a brightly
lit case, Laura sees wigs
in every color. "Wow, I
can have the coolest mane
in town!" she squeals.

13

Lions walk on the balls of their feet instead of their full paws.

Laura struts out of the shop. She is careful not to mess up her new mane. She feels a raindrop. "Uh-oh," she gasps. Soon rain is pouring down.

15

A lion can run for short distances at up to 35 miles per hour and can leap as far as 36 feet.

Leo comes racing down the sidewalk, jumping over puddles. He cries, "What's that soggy thing on your head?"

"Oh Leo," Laura sighs. "I just wanted to have a beautiful mane like yours!"

17

Lions' coats are yellow-gold, and adult males have dark manes. Young lions have spots on their coats.

Leo puts his paw on Laura's shoulder and says, "Laura, don't you know that only boys have big manes? Besides, you are beautiful just the way you are. You don't need a big mane!"

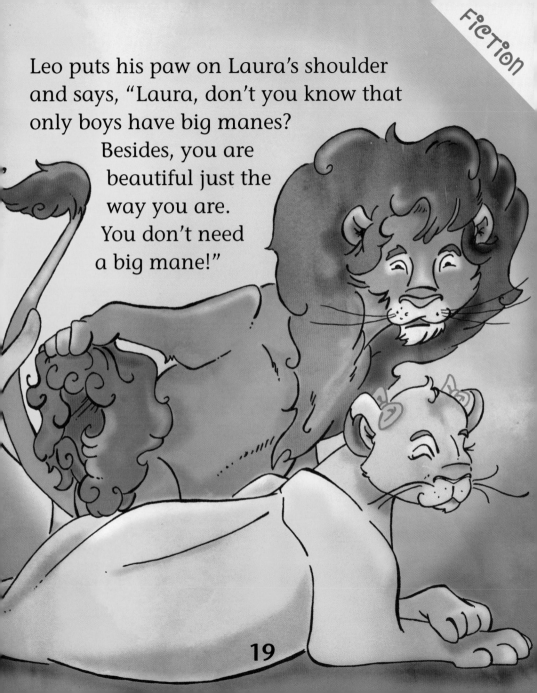

19

FACT OR FICTION?

Read each statement below. Then decide whether it's from the FACT section or the FICTION section!

  1. Lions' long tails help them balance.

  2. Lions eat vegetables.

  3. Lions wear wigs.

 4. Young lions have spots on their coats.

ANSWERS
1. fact 2. fiction 3. fiction 4. fact

Young lion cubs spend a lot of their time playing. 10
Their playing helps them develop survival skills such as 19
stalking and fighting. 22

Lions' long tails help them balance. The lion is the 32
only kind of cat with a tassel at the tip of its tail. 45

Most cats eat standing up, but lions eat crouching 54
or lying down. Lions are carnivores. 60

A lion's roar can be heard up to five miles away. 71
Lions roar to let the other lions in the pride know 82
where they are or to scare off lions that don't belong. 93

Lions' eyes are very large and yellow. They have a 103
special coating that helps lions to see well even when 113
there is little light. 117

Lions walk on the balls of their feet instead of their 128
full paws. 130

A lion can run for short distances at up to 35 miles 142
per hour and can leap as far as 36 feet. 152

Lions' coats are yellow-gold, and adult males have 161
dark manes. Young lions have spots on their coats. 170

Laura and Leo have been best friends since they were young cubs. They learned to pounce, growl, and hunt together. They were very much alike.

Laura hasn't seen Leo all summer, so she can't wait to see him today.

Ring! The doorbell chimes, and Laura leaps to the door. "Hi, Laura!" Leo roars happily.

Laura stares. Leo has a beautiful, new mane! They are not alike anymore.

Laura loves Leo's new look. She decides that if she eats a lot of vegetables, she can grow a mane like Leo's. Laura eats and eats, but she does not grow a mane.

Laura rides her scooter over to Manes on Main, where Harry the hair guru works. "Harry," she cries, "can you help me grow a mane?"

Harry roars with laughter, "Oh Laura, you'll never grow a mane. But you can buy one. Take a look over there."

Inside a brightly lit case, Laura sees wigs in every 156
color. "Wow, I can have the coolest mane in town!" 166
she squeals. 168

Laura struts out of the shop. She is careful not to 179
mess up her new mane. She feels a raindrop. "Uh-oh," 190
she gasps. Soon rain is pouring down. 197

Leo comes racing down the sidewalk, jumping 204
over puddles. He cries, "What's that soggy thing on 213
your head?" 215

"Oh Leo," Laura sighs. "I just wanted to have a 225
beautiful mane like yours!" 229

Leo puts his paw on Laura's shoulder and says, 238
"Laura, don't you know that only boys have big 247
manes? Besides, you are beautiful just the way you 256
are. You don't need a big mane!" 263

GLOSSARY

carnivore. one who eats meat

coat. the fur covering of an animal

growl. to make a deep, low, threatening sound

hunt. to search for, chase, and catch something
to eat

pounce. to jump suddenly on something in order
to catch it

pride. a group of lions that live, travel, and feed
together

survival. the act of staying alive

tassel. a decoration made by gathering loose threads
or cords and tying them at one end or something
that looks like this sort of decoration

To see a complete list of SandCastle™ books and other nonfiction titles from
ABDO Publishing Company, visit www.abdopublishing.com or contact us at:
4940 Viking Drive, Edina, Minnesota 55435 • 1-800-800-1312 • fax: 1-952-831-1632